THE PARK CLEAN-UP

by **Dorothy H Price** illustrated by **Shiane Salabie**

raintree

a Capstone company — publishers for children

Raintree is an imprint of Capstone Global Library Limited,
a company incorporated in England and Wales having its
registered office at 264 Banbury Road, Oxford, OX2 7DY –
Registered company number: 6695582

Edited by Alison Deering
Designed by Jaime Willems
Production by Whitney Schaefer

Design element: Shutterstock: Alexzel, Betelejze,
cuppuccino, wormig

978 1 3982 5323 0

British Library Cataloguing in Publication Data
A full catalogue record for this book is available from the
British Library.

Printed and bound in India.

CONTENTS

MEET JC

Hi! My name is Jalen Corey Pierce, but everyone calls me JC. I am seven years old.

I live with Mum, Dad and my baby sister, Maya. Nana and Pop-Pop live in our block of flats too. So do my two best friends, Amir and Vicky.

My family and I used to live in a small town. Now I live in a big city with tall buildings and lots of people. Come along with me on all my new adventures!

Chapter 1

THE PARK PROBLEM

JC walked to school with
Dad, Amir and Vicky every day.
They passed skyscrapers and
underground stations. They
also passed their local park.

The park needed a clean-up. It was full of litter. Flowers were dying. There were also people living in tents.

"Do those people sleep in the park?" Vicky asked.

Dad nodded. "They must be homeless," he said. "That means they have no home."

"No home!" JC exclaimed.

That made him sad. In his old town, his family had lived in a house. Their flat in the city was smaller, but it was still a home.

"Maybe we can come up with a plan to clean the park *and* help people," JC said.

Dad smiled. "That's a wonderful idea. We can ask other people to volunteer too."

"What's a volunteer?" Amir asked.

"Someone who gives their time to help those in need," Dad explained.

JC had never volunteered before, but he wanted to help.

"We can all be volunteers!" he exclaimed.

Chapter 2

VOLUNTEERS NEEDED

At school, JC and his friends

told their teacher about the park.

"We need volunteers to help

clean it up," JC said.

"I'll help," Mrs Rowe offered. "Let's start with a list of things you want to get done."

"We know we want to pick up litter and plant flowers," Vicky said.

"We want to help the people without homes too," Amir said.

"I volunteer with a group in my area," Mrs Rowe said. "I'm sure they'll help. We can also ask people to donate supplies."

"Like what?" JC asked.

"Socks, hats and gloves," Mrs Rowe explained. "Those are all things that homeless people need, especially when it's cold."

"That sounds like a great
idea," JC agreed.

"Let's do the clean-up next weekend," Mrs Rowe suggested. "That will give us time to get supplies."

JC grinned. "We've got a plan!"

Chapter 3

THINGS TO DO

"We want to clean up the park next weekend," JC told his family after school. "Mrs Rowe will help. She works with a group that helps homeless people."

"I'd love to plant some autumn flowers," Nana offered.

"You know I'll be there," Pop-Pop said.

Amir and Vicky came over later. JC and his friends made a list of things to do. They numbered the tasks. JC added names next to each one.

"That looks like a good list,"
Mum said.

"We need to ask for donations
too," Vicky said.

"Things like warm clothes,"
Amir added.

"Why don't we make a flyer?"
Dad suggested. "We can hang it
in our lobby. People can sign up."

"Then we'll have lots of volunteers," JC said.

The rest of the week was busy. Mrs Rowe talked to her local group. They agreed to help JC and his friends collect donations.

Mum and Dad bought supplies like gloves and bin bags. Nana and Pop-Pop found autumn flowers to plant. At the end of the week, the volunteer list was *full*!

Chapter 4

CLEANING UP

On Saturday, everyone met
at the local park.

"I have bin bags for collecting
litter," Dad said.

"Pop-Pop and I will start planting the flowers," said Nana.

"Maya can help us," said Pop-Pop.

Mrs Rowe came with her volunteer group. They set up a table. JC, Amir and Vicky helped with the donations. People could take what they needed.

Everyone worked hard all day.
When they had finished, the
litter had gone – and so had all
the donations.

"This was a great idea,"
Amir's mum said.

"I'm proud of you kids for wanting to help," Vicky's dad added.

JC and his friends smiled. The park clean-up was a success.

"Thanks to everyone who volunteered!" JC exclaimed.

GLOSSARY

donate give something as a gift

flyer printed piece of paper that tells about an upcoming event

homeless not having a home or place of shelter to live in

litter pieces of paper or other rubbish that are scattered around carelessly

supply item needed in order to do a job or task

task piece of work that needs to be done

volunteer person who offers to do something without pay

BEING A VOLUNTEER

There are many ways to volunteer. What are some things you and your friends could do to help other people where you live? Write a list and add tasks next to each name. Share your list with your parents and see if you can make a change like JC and his friends did!

LET'S TALK

1. Do you go by bus to school or walk like JC? Have you done both? Which do you like best? Why?

2. JC feels sad when he sees homeless people in the park. Have you ever seen homeless people where you live? How did it make you feel?

3. JC, his friends and family decide to help others by volunteering. Have you ever volunteered? What did you do? If not, what would you like to do?

LET'S WRITE

1. Do you think JC, Vicky and Amir will volunteer again? List some other ways they could help in their local area.

2. JC asked for help to make his idea work. Have you ever needed help from others? Try writing a list of people who you could ask to help.

3. JC and his friends collected items like socks, hats and gloves. What else do you think they could have collected? Write a list of items.

Dorothy H Price loves writing stories for young readers. Her first picture book, *Nana's Favorite Things*, is proof of that. Dorothy was a 2019 winner of the We Need Diverse Books Mentorship Program in the United States. She hopes all young readers know they can grow up to write stories too.

Shiane Salabie is a Jamaica-born illustrator based in Philadelphia, USA. When she moved to the United States, she discovered her first true love: the library. Shiane later realized that she wanted to bring stories to life and uses her art to do so.